Soon To Be A
Major Motion Picture

Judith Arcana

Staff

Kimberly Brown, Executive Editor
Lindsey Grudnicki, Assistant Editor
Michelle Orr, Creative Director
Nicole Rollender, Editor
Emily Shearer, Poetry Editor
Mari Ann Stefanelli, Copy Editor
Cindy Orna, Layout Designer

Minerva Rising is an independent literary journal celebrating the creativity and wisdom in every woman. We publish thought-provoking fiction, creative nonfiction, original prints, photography, graphic art, essays and poetry by women writers and artists. Subscriptions are $32 US for one year (three issues). Minerva Rising accepts unsolicited manuscripts and artwork that addresses our current theme. Please visit our website at www.minervarising. com for detailed information on the theme for our next issue and our submission guidelines.

Minerva Rising's first prose chapbook asked for submissions that speak creatively, powerfully, thoughtfully—and maybe even uniquely—to the theme "Daring to be the Woman I Am."

A special thanks to Rosemary Daniell for judging the contest. Her commitment to encouraging women to write their truth continues to inspire all that we do.

MINERVA RISING
literary journal

Acknowledgements

Much gratitude to Daniel Arcana, Jonathan Arlook, Lantz Arroyo, Peaches Bass, Sarah Boehm, Andrea Carlisle, Cindy Cooper, Jodi Darby, Megan Felling, Nicole Hollander, Jan Johnson, Gwyn Kirk, Stephanie Poggi, BT Shaw, Kate Weck and Erin Yanke. I'm also grateful to the Mesa Refuge, the Wurlitzer Foundation, Soapstone and Milepost5, all of which gave me time and space to write – and to the artists whose work inspires the tattoo content in all my Jane stories: the late Cliff Raven and Buddy McFall in Chicago, Lyle Tuttle in San Francisco, and Mary Jane Haake in Portland, Oregon.

Dedication

This chapbook is dedicated to the memory of Grace Paley,
who created some of the best short stories ever written in
American English, and used much of the energy, passion
and power of her eighty-four years doing serious street-level
political action.

Author's Note

This chapbook is fiction that's been drawn from life and invented. The style and content express my literary and political influences, both my experience doing underground/illegal abortion work and my experience writing (like coloring) outside the lines. Reading Grace Paley, an American master of short fiction, helped me understand I don't have to use quotation marks for dialogue, and I don't have to make up "transitions" when moving from one place or character to another (about that, Grace said: *I just like to take a big jump*).

Soon To Be A Major Motion Picture

I remember tiny details and I remember whole scenes.
Sometimes I even see them as shots, as if through a camera
lens – like the scene with Shelley, the woman I was with when
we got busted: We're standing there, waiting for the elevator,
and the camera is behind us – so when the doors open, the
audience sees the cops in that frame. Those guys looked like
they were *already* in a movie, actors playing 1972 Chicago cops:
white guys, shiny black shoes, trench coats. They talked like
they learned how from TV.

But here's the thing – there's a lot I don't remember. I don't
remember the name of any other woman that day, just Shelley,
and I don't remember what I said on the phone when I called
my husband, Eli, from the police station and got Tony, his
partner. I've forgotten a lot. We'll have to invent all that –
doesn't matter though, does it? There's the mystery of memory
itself, for one thing. Who knows, now, what really happened
that day, or might have happened? For the movie, it'll be *based
on a true story*. It can't *be* a true story; that's impossible. If it's

good though, I mean if we make a really good movie, it'll tell the truth.

I've got files here on my laptop – my research, a bunch of pieces I've written over the years. When we decided to meet, I put it all together, making a list of possible scenes. I've never worked on a fiction film, never wrote a screenplay or a treatment. I spent some time a few years ago thinking maybe I'd do it, but that did not – to put it kindly – pan out.

Now, don't be offended: I'm using this little recorder. My agent told me to do it so I'd have my own copy, audio, of what goes on here today. She said we were far enough along that I could talk freely but I should record everything. And this'll be clearly visible in your video, so we'll have a cross-referencing thing going on. After all the weeks of email and phone conversation – and seeing films you've worked on – I feel like I know you. It's probably an anachronism for me to even *care* about knowing you outside of cyberspace, but that's who I am, that's who you're working with here.

So, you don't mind if I'm sort of all over the place? After each question, I'll just talk 'til I stop? Then you'll ask more questions and I'll talk some more.

I remember two women from the holding tank, when the seven of us, the Janes, got put in with them. Even right now, while I'm telling you this, I can see both women *clearly*. It's weird, isn't it, what we remember? And what we don't? The first time I tried to write this, I didn't know who took care of the baby while I was working. Which is truly bizarre because at the time, I couldn't stop thinking about the baby. There was the breast milk situation plus fear – I was thinking: What if they take my baby away because I've been arrested? And: If I do time, he won't know me. That was in my head all day, and it was a *long* day; we started doing abortions about nine, got busted at three, got to the lockup around midnight.

Scenes and characters. It's gotta be different, thinking about scenes and characters for *film*. I mean different from writing stories and poems – what I do. Like this: the woman who fingerprinted me is the one who took me to the cell, and then, later, to see the lawyers, and down to the holding pen again, before night court – we had a miniature relationship by the end of the night, you know? Writing about her, I gave her a name, Angie, and I wrote lines for her, some from what could be memory. She was kind to me, and I made her a character. Now though, we might not have her in there at all. I need to learn from you how to think about this, how to make decisions for a movie.

For structure, form, I think of Barthelme – he has that great story where abortion docs talking about their work are mashed up with other characters at a fancy dress ball. In film, that'd maybe be Jarmusch? The messiness of it, everything happening at once – real life! It's hard enough to decide which people and scenes to use; then we have to fold 'em together to get the effect we want, the *effect* of real life. That's true in most movies, don't you think? Not just in collage forms like *Crash* or *Mind the Gap* but even the more story-telling kind. *Monsoon Wedding*!

We have to decide whether our movie is the kind where the audience knows about the bust early or the kind where it's more like a mystery, an adventure where they don't know what'll happen. Most people *won't* know this story, coming in. It's not a piece of history people are familiar with. So do we start by giving them that knowledge? Do we use flashbacks? Maybe surround the story of the bust with other stories of the abortion service? Stories of that year and time, pre-Roe but on the way to Roe? Do we want to have a present-day moment to move back from, or is it all in the seventies? Do we want to show the time when funding got cut – the Hyde amendment or when everybody finally recognized that Roe was now irrelevant, eviscerated? Should we show Roe going down?

Another thing, also structural, but in another way: You know how, in *American Splendor*, they did that fusion, that combination of fiction and documentary plus the combination of animation and live action? They used animation because they were dealing with a comic book person – Pekar – so it was a natural, however unusual. But other movies that have no obvious or special reason do that, too – mix methods, I mean. Like *Juno*, in the credit sequence. Oh hey, even better – better than *Juno* – is *Run Lola Run*! Structurally fascinating, structural play that never takes you away from the action, the characters. It even deepens them, really. Way tougher than *Juno*. Really, given our material, I think it's worth considering. I'm not suggesting we do anything as, like, *cubist* as Todd Haynes did in his Dylan movie. (Wasn't that brilliant?) I'm just thinking we could have some formal schtick, something structurally notable. That could be good. I don't want to make a huge case for animation – it'd just be fun. But, fact is, this is *history*, about real people, and there's a documentary with footage we could use. That's a good argument for fusion, don't you think? I've got the DVD here, in case we need to refer to it.

We should probably think about doing what they did in the first *If These Walls* – when the Demi Moore character approximates the death pose from that classic photograph of a woman who had a butcher abortion. Even before they caught the Philadelphia guy in 2011, a thing like that would reverberate in the audience – that mix of fiction and reality, layering and complicating. Good movies are complicated, right? Like real life.

Some of the original characters and situations might fall away; I saw that when I was working on my own. We don't have to include everything, even in a movie about things that really happened. I am *not* suggesting we change history, though – that's outrageous. Look what they did to the history of England in the first Cate Blanchett *Elizabeth*! I am *not* in favor of that. Like, I wouldn't change the date of the bust, or the location.

Conflate characters? Maybe. Sure. When I'm doing fiction, after all, inventing characters, they're made of everything I know – that's big conflation. Janes? You mean, would I conflate the Janes who were busted, have four or five, not seven? I don't think so. In the group, the whole Service, sure – but not the seven; there *were* seven, there have to *be* seven. That, for me, is like changing the year, the city – changing history. I once heard about a TV show using the Service. A woman I met in a bathroom line in DC at the big march in 2004 told me about it when she saw my JANE button. She said the abortions on that show were done by docs, and the docs were men – or at least one was. And the whole scene was Pittsburgh or some other place, not Chicago. Definitely out of the question.

Yeah, I *have* thought about doing those parallel tracks: Sarah Weddington and her team, working on the Roe case – not actually connected with the Service; they probably heard about the bust in spring of '72 and, like anybody who cares about this, they had to be affected by it. So they *could* be in it. I'm not saying they *should*. The Seven were definitely affected by those lawyers, their work. After all, the Janes got released on bail and their case got dropped eight months later – and why? Because of Roe moving through the system to the Court. Having our case dropped and our records declared "expunged," that's a link between the Weddington story and ours. So it's a connection that could be used, or mentioned, in the movie. Or not.

Yeah, that's right. We always called it the Service. I know pretty much everybody who learned about us later calls the whole group JANE or sometimes "the Jane collective" – but we didn't. It was the Abortion Counseling Service of the Chicago Women's Liberation Union – which we also didn't call it. We had to shorten it – obviously – and used the one word. We did call ourselves Janes, and we played with the word, called the work "Jane-ing" and, at some point, like two years in, started calling a couple of the necessary jobs "big Jane" and "little Jane" – phone work, counseling assignments, making appointments. Lots of us did those jobs, sort of in rotation, over the years. Oh – and this: we were *not* a collective. We'll see what happens, as our work develops, whether we want to even deal with the politics of that – like how that concept got applied to the Janes by the next generations.

It's interesting how language changes. Like in the video documentary – it came out in '95 – one Jane (she's dead now) actually calls women who came through the Service "clients," a word un-thought of in those years, and certainly a word she, that Jane, would never have used *then*. It would have been wrong, in our thinking and practice, to separate them from us, to *professionalize* the Janes. We were too raggedy-ass for that and committed to a way of thinking about the work that basically damns such separation. We were women who learned how to do some necessary technical work, and we understood that most women who needed that work could do it, too – if they wanted to learn. Positions taken around the speculum could switch at any time. And they did. There were always Janes who joined up after coming through the Service to get their abortions.

Anyway. Let's set aside Women's Studies 201 and get back to the movies.

You realize I'm telling this from my own memory *and* what I've gathered from other people's memories about that time? There's no separation any more. When I decided to work on these stories again, to write more about the Service, I made a rule for myself: I wouldn't watch the video documentary again until I was done, and I wouldn't re-read anybody's Jane writing either, until I had complete drafts of my own stories. Not necessarily polished, but complete. I wanted to draw everything up, like from a well, a pool of fluid memories. After that I could make up things – write fiction, not memoir.

When I write fiction, about anything, I'm already doing the same thing you're getting from me in this interview. I probably *couldn't* tell it all in straight chronological order anyway, so it's great you're willing to be loose. While I'm talking, things make me think of other things. I did make a list though, a rough chronology of that day – May 3, 1972. I've got it here, brought it with me. Just in case.

Thank you, yes, I'll need some water. No, no coffee. You made a good choice here. I'm so glad this big suite has that tiny kitchen. Not only do we have lots of room to spread out, we've got coffee, tea and a place to brew it.

One person who comes to mind is Francesca – I named her that, don't know if I ever knew her real name – the one who called the cops. She could be a character. I wrote a few sentences for her. She says:

> **It's a sin; she can't do this. She has to have it; we all have to. Jesus doesn't want her to get rid of this baby. That's why I did it.**

For the movie we could have her say those lines in court or maybe in a scene at the police station: A Jane sees her, this woman who'd been among those waiting at the front, sees she's being talked to by the cops real intently – different from the others, you know?

We never knew if she made the call on her own or was part of a group. One way or another, most of us thought that our own cops, in the precincts where we usually worked, wouldn't have acted on her call. They never did before; this was the only bust, ever, in more than four years, and they knew all about us. They knew who we were and where we were. They knew we were good, clean, didn't hurt anybody, and weren't in it for the money. They didn't even come after us when that reporter (what was her name? I've got her in my notes) wrote an exposé for *The Reader* (you have that, right?). Sometimes the cops used the Service for their own daughters, wives, girlfriends – or so I've been told.

When we were brought in, the seven of us, somebody actually said – What are we doing *here*? This isn't our neighborhood – these aren't even our cops! I was a northsider so they wouldn't have been my cops anyway, but I did a lot of time in Hyde Park for abortion work, so I knew what that meant. Those Cottage Grove guys, they were strangers.

Here's my thinking. I made up "Angie" and "Francesca" – as if I created the people, as if they weren't, hadn't ever been, real. It seemed like the natural thing to do, appropriate for fiction, melding real life (or what the writer/movie maker *thinks* is real life) with what we make up, what we invent on purpose. We're not talking James Frey here; this is not about being phony or "lying" – in any ethical/moral sense. This is what Grace Paley meant when she said a story is a lie the writer tells in order to tell the truth.

So none of these people has a real name. I changed all the names but my own; I'm still Denah. It's simpler, easier, safer all 'round, even though I go in and out of the frame all the time in my mind. Talking about myself in the third person *can* get confusing, especially when I'm trying to be coherent for somebody else, like now.

Writing alone, before you contacted me, I decided to have the guy who sets up the bust become a character. Maybe he's got S. Epatha Merkerson's job on *Law and Order*, but in 1972 Chicago you can bet he'd be a white man. He testified that Denah lost them three times, driving from the front to the place. (I *loved* hearing him say that in court.)

If we do make him a character, I think this guy should have a conscious position on abortion. He could be something of a pragmatist, philosophically speaking. Like, he personally thinks the woman should be the decision maker, but he's an officer of the law and abortion's against the law, the Janes are breaking the law – all that.

That's different from my own cop, Denah's cop – *his* attitude about abortion I haven't decided yet, though we may not need one for him. His attitude about me, and how he decided to approach the arrest interview, is in some things I published a while back, a few years before we first talked about doing this. Have you gotten to that stuff yet? I have it here, in one of these folders.

Yeah, here's Denah-the-character and her cop: Denah's put in an office alone, still handcuffed, with the cuffs locked onto an iron ring attached to the wall. What? Yes. Really. She could sort of hear Claudia and Betsy's voices; the doors weren't closed, and they were in an office next door or across the hall. She's sitting on a wooden chair near, but not at, a big wooden desk, and the cuffs, the metal kind, are cutting into her skin. She's at an awkward angle, and her arms are raised, hanging from the ring on the wall. She'd been locked onto a similar hookup inside the police van. The office is warm, overheated in fact; but the van was cold – cold air, cold metal that made her shudder. Eight years later, when my son Joey got hit by a car, and I was in the back of the ambulance holding him, I felt his body shudder that same way – police vans, ambulances, they're all cold metal, and lots of people who get put inside them are in shock. So they get that stammering kind of shiver, a hard shiver.

Anyway. So: the cuffs, the iron ring. She's sitting there thinking it's overkill, sorta medieval. But she doesn't know if it's mindlessness, meanness or strategy on their part. Her cop is sitting at the big desk, making notes, deliberately not looking at her, maybe tactically ignoring her. She's watching him, thinking about how to talk to him, what words and tone to use. And knowing definitely that soon she will have to pee. Here's how I wrote that part:

He's wearing a yellow short sleeve dress shirt with a black knit necktie and tan pants. No visible badge. He's a white guy with bright black hair cut too short, a slightly military effect. There's a shield tattooed on his left forearm; it looks new to Denah, who got her first tattoo maybe six or eight months ago. She thinks he's a couple years under thirty, about her age. He looks up, makes eye contact. He stands, comes around the desk, takes the cuffs off the iron ring and unlocks the cuffs from her wrists.

She slumps in relief, rubs her wrists and says, I need to go to the bathroom.

He walks her to the door of a nearby women's room, waits outside. When they're back in the office, he opens a manila folder, reads silently, then looks at her across the desk – eye contact again – and says, I see you were a high school teacher. I used to be a high school Biology teacher.

She says, I taught English, Humanities and Creative Writing – but you must have all that in your folder. What made you give it up? You didn't exactly move to a higher paying job, did you? Cops and teachers, serving the public with small paychecks, right?

He laughs. He lights a cigarette and offers it to her right from his mouth. She takes it, says, Camels, my dad's brand. She puts it in her mouth, then pulls it out and says, Forgot – I'm off it.

He smiles. Then he says, Yeah, this salary isn't what they call "compelling." But you didn't move up the class ladder either, did you? We couldn't find any money at your place, and the only woman who's been willing to say *anything* says she paid $43. I don't see you flying down to Rio on your cut. But I'll be getting a solid pension; you probably can't say the same. I guess we'll have to assume you did it for some other reason. Right?

She looks directly into his eyes. Did what?

That scene is one of the ones solidified in my mind as what happened that day. He had information about me because I was in the news in 1970 when I got fired from my teaching job.

What? Oh, the usual reasons for those years: two other teachers and I were accused, like Socrates, of corrupting the youth with our words and thoughts. Actually, the stated complaints were that we didn't follow the curriculum guide and rules about attendance and grades. It was all about politics, though, everybody knew that. Teachers were being fired all over the country, a lot of parents were freaked out – this was when the phrase "generation gap" got invented. But that's a whole 'nother movie.

Anyway, our conversation was not what I'd expect to be talking about over there at the cop shop – if I'd expected to be busted for abortion, which I definitely hadn't.

Hmm? Oh, sure, yes, the Janes talked about it, how to act, what to do; the idea was you'd never go to work without a contact number to call, but I didn't think it was inevitable. No. In my mind, for sure, it was *not* inevitable.

Sitting there, arrested on dozens of felony charges – when abortion's illegal it's classified as felony homicide – his attention to my personal history and the revelation of his own snagged my interest. Maybe that's why he did it. Biology, I was thinking, so he must know all about this. That was silly of me, when you realize how many of them don't know a damn thing about women. But it is what I thought.

In one draft – written longhand quite a while ago – I wrote:

The dogwood was in bloom and the flowering plum. Chicago has spring for only about a week each year, mostly going nonstop from the darkened patches of snow on street corners to a sticky heat so intense some people sit outside on the stoop all night.

He was wearing a necktie in the humid Chicago springtime, when the skin on students' arms had begun to stick to the pocked varnish of their wooden desktops at South Shore and DuSable, Roosevelt and VonSteuben, to the slippery formica on newer desks at Mather and Mother Guerin – reminding them that summer school was going to be hell.

He'd been a teacher, like me, and he, too, had changed jobs. Neither of us had gone up in salary, but both of us were doing what we thought was *good work*.

What's interesting here is that Denah liked the guy, even though she knew he was her adversary, dangerous to her and the other women. She liked him as a person, *a human*.

Here's some backstory for the Denah character: she takes time off when her baby's born, and when he's a few months old, she goes back to work, returning to her medical training as an abortionist and doing other Service work, sort of part-time. She's already learned and done long terms, she's learning to do D&Cs. Her first full-time workday is the day they get cracked.

Denah's the driver that day, in a borrowed Ford station wagon, going back and forth between the front in Hyde Park (brown brick 6-flat) and the place in South Shore (grey highrise by the lake). She took three, four or five women each time, using different routes, pulling over to collect the money with each group. I have some memory fragments – like asking them to be quiet in the hall at the place, bringing them in, and introducing them to Paula and Harriet.

Oh, here's something: There was a woman who was done, and Denah was taking her group back to the front, but she said, I gotta lie down for a while longer – I don't wanna go back yet. When I get back there, to my husband, I'll have to smile and be cool, and I'm not ready to do that – you know what I mean? I don't remember her whole face, but I know she had a tiny open space between her two front teeth; I saw that when she smiled at me. She was wearing a thin grey cardigan with a rolled collar. Jeez! I haven't had that memory come up for forty years!

The thing about actually being arrested – that word is so right, if you think about how it means *stopped, held in place* – we, Shelley and I, were certainly *arrested*.

The arrest itself, my part of it, went like this (and we should definitely use this) – Denah's out in the hall with Shelley because she asks to be taken back to the front soon as she's done. Shelley says:

> **My daughter's over in Children's Memorial today, she's only two, she's having an operation on her stomach valve. It doesn't work right, since she was born. My husband's over there, with her, for that, while I'm here, for this. Could I leave right after I'm done? Could you take me back right away? Would that be okay? Would the other women mind, do you think?**

> **Denah looks at her copy of the day's list and says, Sure, why not? I can do that, I'll take you back as soon as you're done.**

So around three o'clock they're standing out in the hall in front of the elevator. The elevator doors open, and these men get off. Denah and Shelley step aside to let them pass, but then – here's a place we have to make up what happened because the actual moment, the details of it, are not in my memory. Isn't that weird? You'd think that moment would be at the top of the list, but no. We don't have to worry, though because isn't that one of the most common scenes in TV and movies – that moment? You could write it with only half your IQ in gear, couldn't you? How they're arrested, stopped by these guys, these TV-type cops? And if you don't know the old procedures, we can go back to *Dragnet* – no, no, wait, that's too early, we need whatever it was right then, 1972, to avoid anachronism. I hope you care about that. I care about that.

Were cop shows big in the late sixties, early seventies, like they are now? That was when I pretty much stopped watching TV. What *was* on then? We can find out on the Net – or in my office; I've got this great book that lists movies and tv shows and headlines and fashions and inventions and sports for almost a hundred years. The writer's friend.

What I do have in my memory (or I already made this up and now I can't tell the difference) is that soon as the initial moment of confusion passes, and realization takes hold, Shelley starts crying. This is in the hallway, away from the elevators, where the two women are being held. Denah comforts her, puts an arm around her, tells her she doesn't have to say anything, counsels her about her rights. Hearing Denah say those things, the cops separate them, and one guy takes her downstairs because they decide Denah's a "perpetrator" and Shelley's a "victim." Outside, Denah's cuffed and left locked in a police van. She's alone, scared and shaking inside that cold metal van the way I said before.

I have no memory of ever seeing Shelley again – not at the station, not in court, nowhere. I sometimes wonder if they maybe let her go. She was frightened, thinking about her little girl in the hospital – and they didn't need her. Maybe they realized, with all those other people, they didn't even need her.

They must've had several cops and paddy wagons at the front too, for rounding up all the women who'd come for abortions, and all the mothers, sisters, children, fathers, husbands, friends and lovers who were waiting for them – my memory's got the number forty-three in it, but who knows? At the station, it seems to me, there was a fairly large open waiting area and all those people. Everybody from the front and everybody from the place was there. The children were over-tired, hungry, running around. Poor little kids.

And there was a place where we made our phone calls – maybe a bank of pay phones in a hallway? This is a period piece we're doing, might as well be 1872 because think how different it is *now* – with abortion so recently illegal again – everybody carrying cell phones with cameras and email and text-messaging. A bust like this'll be out on the Net, YouTubed before anybody even gets booked!

So, anyway, in that open space where the phones are, the Janes all see each other for the first time since they were brought in. I don't know whether the separate interviews or the group meeting out in the open comes first – which makes sense for the movie? I do know that at first the cops weren't sure which people they'd rounded up were abortionists – "suspects" or "crooks" in their terms. In my case, since there's only one driver and they'd followed me, and then saw Shelley and me at the elevator door, heard her cry and heard me tell her about her rights – they didn't have much to decide. But they did have to bob and weave to figure out which other women were Janes.

Some chronology: They take their wagonloads from the front and the place to the Cottage Grove station and then, after a long time there, they take us – the seven – to the women's lockup, downtown. Don't remember how we got there. Paddy wagon, wouldn't you think, another van? I have no memory of that passage. There, when we were booked, one of the guards – I think they were called matrons – was a big woman with soft skin. She's the woman I called Angie when I wrote this part:

Angie touches Denah's elbow to steer her around. Her hair is metal-grey, blunt-cut short, and she's got a faded eagle tattoo, wings spread around her right wrist; she smells like lit cigarettes. She tells Denah how to roll her fingertips so the prints won't smudge and hands her a coarse paper towel for the slime that

gets the ink off. She hangs a numbered plate around Denah's neck when she directs her to stand still and turn sideways for the mug shots.

She guides Denah to the cells, a set-up like office cubicles at an insurance company, only this big room has a concrete floor and a really high ceiling and glaring lights overhead. The cells are arranged in groups with narrow lanes between them. They have metal doors and walls, and their ceilings are like sections of chain link fence, painted black and laid down on top of metal boxes. The walls don't go all the way down; they're like the walls in a public toilet, and there's a constant draft at floor level. It's after midnight.

Angie's gruff decency is in her voice when she says, I'll put you in with your partner. She unlocks a cell and points Denah into it with her chin. Denah's puzzled until the door swings open and Linda, a new young Jane she'd met at the front that morning, jumps up to embrace her. Linda's about 18, a college student working the front her first time that day. She'd been alone in the cell before Angie brought Denah. All around them women are banging on the metal walls, wailing, screaming; their banshee voices ricochet in the big room.

Six Janes in pairs were in three cells in a row; they could talk, call out, confer and reassure each other. This is how they know one's missing. Turns out, they learn later, Harriet's parents have called the state's Republican senator, to get him to do whatever it is he does for such people in situations like this. Denah thinks Harriet must be embarrassed, and maybe frightened, to be separated from the others and alone. But she barely knows Harriet, who joined when Denah was out, having Joey.

After a while, the cell-to-cell talking over the walls stops. Linda and Denah take inventory. Their cell is maybe nine by five feet. There's a slab of wood attached to one metal wall; it's about six feet long and eighteen inches wide, for sitting – or sleeping if the luck of exhaustion shuts out noise and light. There's a filthy little sink and toilet at one end. Denah milks her breasts into the sink for relief. Their communication moves from silence to wisecracks to worries, then back to silence.

That's what I've got for that part.

Hmm? Yeah, you could say that. I *was* exhausted – and scared, angry, physically uncomfortable. I think about it this way: On that day I moved freely when I started out, traveling from the

North Side to South Side, driving back and forth between the front and the place. Then I was constrained, held – *arrested*: in the hallway of the apartment building and the police van, the office at the Cottage Grove station, the holding tank and cell at 11th and State. I was in another cell, too, and in night court (a room in the building's basement, shabby but with one of those high platforms so the judge can look down on you). I got back to my own street a few hours past dawn. I think the whole experience was just about twenty-four hours – and thinking that way renders it, *that day*, almost surreal. For me.

The holding tank. Yeah, there's a story there, and I'll tell you, but wait. Here's what happened at 3 am when Angie took me out of the cell. She guided me to a tiny dark room – another kind of cell. In my memory it's steel mesh, a cage. I could see guys in suits inside.

Oh, hey, listen, I have the mug shots, we can use them if we want. We got 'em when our records were supposedly expunged.

What? Well, I say it that way because I sure don't believe the Chicago Police or the federal government actually *destroy* anybody's records, especially in cases with overt political implications. I bet they had a stamp that says EXPUNGED, and a place where they stored everything stamped that way, a place for storing supposedly-destroyed files. No such worries now – data storage is forever, if you want it to be.

Those pictures – my hair was pretty long then, twisted back and clipped to keep it out of the way for work. I'm wearing Levi's, or maybe cords, and a dark sweatshirt, probably sneakers though I can't be sure. I know my feet were cold in that cell; a damp wind came in under the metal walls and swirled around the concrete floor, moving all the time, like there was a fan somewhere, or an open window.

Thing is, my breasts had been filling since I nursed the baby that morning. I'd been assuming I'd have a chance to empty them at least once – and figured I'd be home by five or six. But I hadn't gotten to it yet when the trenchcoats got off the elevator. So when I leaned over that dirty little sink in the corner of our cell and kneaded my engorged breasts to get them soft enough to release, it'd been about sixteen hours. Not good.

Wait a minute. Where was I going here? …. Ah. Right, okay, thanks – I was going to talk about what happened when Angie took me out of the cell.

She led me to a tiny dark room like a cage. It's after three in the morning and these lawyers are waiting. They stand up when Angie brings me in: one is Tony, my husband, Eli's, law partner, a guy I've known for years, a real sweetheart; one is Al, a nice guy who went to law school with them – very smart, well-connected; and one is Hank, who used to hit on me when Eli wasn't around. I thought these guys must know about the baby.

I wrote this part a while ago and still have some of the draft. Denah says:

Where's my baby? Who's with Joey?

Tony immediately puts his hand on her shoulder, pulls out a chair for her and says, Eli's home. He's with Joey. She slides down into the chair, closes her eyes. Nobody says anything.

Denah looks up, sits up, says, And where's Harriet? Where the hell is Harriet? Do you know she's not with the rest of us? We're all together back there except her.

They tell her Harriet's in another section of the jail and explain how Senator Percy's office has gotten a lawyer who'll work separately on her case – she will not be part of the seven for legal purposes. That's all I remember about that business and, like I said, it may not be useful in the movie anyway. Maybe it's even inaccurate. The folks who worked in the senator's office back then are unlikely to corroborate anyhow.

Al, who seems to be captain of this little team, leans forward, elbows on the table, and says, Here's the plan, Denah: We want to take you out, now, down to night court. We believe the night court judge will set low bail and let you out tonight because 1) we know the guy, 2) you're a nice white lady married to a lawyer, and 3) you're a nursing mother! Really we should need only that, but we've got all three going for us. He smiles at her.

When she doesn't smile back, he says, Point is, if we do this now, when the other Janes get to court in the morning, whoever *that* judge is will have to set low bail, too – your precedent will call for it because of our guy's decision, the night court judge.

She looks at them; they're looking at her. She can see how, even tired, they're excited. Adrenaline up, like at a demonstration. Or a football game. Hank reaches across the table to take her hand; Denah pulls back. She looks at Tony. Then she says she doesn't want to be separated from the others, says she has to think about it, says she has to ask the other Janes.

At this point, I wrote some text I almost deleted but wound up just setting aside, to use some other time – or never. It's a sub-plot thing about Denah's marriage: She and Eli had an agreement he wouldn't go out of town on days she did Service work. But he flew to NYC for the day and didn't tell her. She finds out when she calls from the Cottage Grove station and gets Tony on the phone. The marriage is rocky anyway, so there's all that. First I decided none of it was necessary for the arrest plot. Then I thought maybe I'd create a subplot for each of the seven – Harriet's got the rich parents thing going on, Paula could have a boyfriend or roommate she lied to about being in the Service – you know what I mean. Then I thought – hey, seven subplots? Totally nuts. I set it all aside, and that's where it is at the moment. But if we want any of it, I've got it.

So, okay, she won't do what they want. The men are disappointed. Denah is obdurate. Hank yells, Guard! and Angie comes to take her back.

In the hall, Angie looks at her and says, You okay?

Walking back to the cells, Denah's thinking, Claudia's a mother – she's got _two_ kids. And Mandy's a mother, too.

When the door clangs, Linda jumps up from the wooden bench to take Denah's hands. They stand there, holding hands, and Denah calls: Janes! Here's what's happening: the lawyers say I should

come with them, now, down to night court in the basement. They think they can get me out for low bail because I'm a nursing mother.

She's embarrassed to tell them the other things Al said.

They say doing this will make low bail for all of you in the morning. I need to know what you think, what you want. Should I do it?

The four Janes in adjacent cells respond instantly, calling out: Are you crazy? Go! Go now! Of course you should go! Get out of here! Go home!

Claudia says, I'd go if I could.

Linda, who realizes she'll be alone or worse when Denah leaves, doesn't say anything. She lets go of Denah's hands.

Women in other cells shout: Who's Jane? Who's getting out? Let *me* out! Some bang on their cell walls, making sheetmetal thunder.

Angie, who's been waiting for the decision, opens the cell and takes her out again. Denah calls: I'm

**going! I'm going to the lawyers! If I don't come
back, you'll know they were right, and the judge let
me go.**

Angie says, This judge has been around a long time.

And that's it, so far, for that scene. Now – here's something
I want you to know: the woman who was that girl, Linda, the
youngest one, the new Jane Denah got put in with – if *she* were
telling you this story, she'd say: Listen, Denah couldn't *wait*
to get out that night, she was *eager* to leave. Linda might even
think Denah suggested the idea herself.

I'm not sure why I think this – some other Jane told me
maybe? Maybe the Linda woman said it in an interview? I don't
know, but it's what my character thinks. Even if it isn't what
the real woman thinks, it works, doesn't it? So we should have
that.

After all, she must've been scared, or pissed off – or both,
when I left her alone in that cell. I never knew her, only in the
months after the bust, when the seven had to meet to deal
with the case. When I saw her, years later, she was less than
interested in relating to me. Once, it was when the video first
came out, she didn't even say hello when she saw me. In any
case, it's good to have her perspective in contrast to mine. I
was surprised by it – but there it is. Conflict! Just what all the

screenwriting teachers call for. And besides, like Dylan said: *To live outside the law, you must be honest.*

Hey, should we use that song? Just that little piece of it? I've thought of several songs for the sound track – I've got a list. A Malvina Reynolds song, a great bit by Melissa Etheridge, something by Tupac, some ani difranco …. Okay. Right. Later for that. Music later. Okay.

Anyway, here's how I ended that section:

> **It's so late when they finally walk out of the building that the morning papers are stacked in the lobby. The headlines on the** *Daily News,* *Trib* **and** *Sun-Times* **say:** *Seven Women Arrested in Abortion Ring* **and** *Underground Abortion Linked to Women's Lib* **and** *Nursing Mother Arrested For Abortion.* **That one has a picture of Denah from two years before, when it ran under a headline saying** *Fired Teachers Called Radicals By School Board.*

I need to drink some water.

Now, here comes a part that's embarrassing, but damn, it'll be great for the movie. Instead of going right home to her baby when the judge lets her out, she has breakfast with the lawyers at a fancy restaurant by the river. I have some text for this, stuff I wrote a while back.

Leaving night court in self-congratulatory celebration mode, the guys say, Hey, let's get some breakfast! Denah, when's the last time you ate? You must be starving. Let's feed Denah!

But she's not hungry. She's exhausted. She's dulled out from stress. She doesn't answer. She stands there on the sidewalk, thick, like a bull surrounded by picadors. They urge her – they'll treat her, they'll take her someplace terrific, someplace new, great food, she'll love it.

She owes them. She knows they don't want to drive her home now; that'd shut down their triumph with anticlimax. She's in a weakened condition *and* she's flattered to be the star of their little show. The tension in her body has been ebbing, but out there on the sidewalk, she's suddenly charged with a shot of adrenaline from, from – from what? Being free in bright yellow sunlight? The exuberance of those grinning guys in their super-charged political moment? Whatever it is, she says, Yes! Let's eat! Feed me!

She may have had Eggs Benedict – or, in her case, Benedict *Arnold.* Oh, maybe it was thick French toast with real maple syrup – let's make it something luxurious to deepen her shame when it hits, later. I don't remember what she ate, but if we use this bit, let's go that way.

They get all the papers and read them out at the table, opening the pages over toast and bacon, butter and marmalade in little ceramic pots. She fades while they crow, quoting bits from various reporters. Her eyes are closed by the time they pay the check, and she's not really awake when she crawls into Al's car, crumpling up on the back seat.

Home, she goes to the baby's room and finds him sleeping. She stands beside the crib, silent. In a few minutes, Joey wakes up, maybe from the smell of her, the smell of her milk. Nursing him, the stress drains out of her body with the milk, liquefying. It's leaving her body in palpable waves, sliding down her arms, her legs, neck and back. She feels the pulse in her fingertips, mingling with the rhythm of Joey's suckling. She hears his small breathing when his mouth falls away from her nipple.

Denah wants to be excused, wants to be *forgiven* for going to breakfast with the lawyers instead of going home. Who has the power to excuse her? Who can forgive her? Certainly not Eli, who betrayed their agreement. Not her parents. The six other Janes?

**She won't discuss it with them – some of them are
practically strangers, after all. Maybe Joey. But he's
too little, too young to exercise power that way. She'll
have to do it herself – and she does, but not for a
long time.**

Nah. No, I don't feel ashamed of it. Now, it's so much *less*, a
lesser offense, in terms of my own laws, my rules and regs for
behavior. I'm *embarrassed* to tell this little story about myself
(I'm happy to hand it off to a character, I will say that), but
I don't feel *shame*. It was a thousand years ago and on a life
scale, that breakfast doesn't weigh much; it's become a petty
infraction. I've done worse, and luckily I've done better. I've
done *way* better most of the time.

It could be good for the movie, though; let's see what happens
as we develop the script – because, really, it's more complicated
than that, the cause of Denah's shame. It's not only this thing
I just told you. It's not that simple. It's connected to what
happens with a woman from the holding tank scene – so let
me tell that now: in my memory, when we first got to the
women's lockup, we were put in a holding tank with two other
women. Actually, I don't remember if they were there when we
got there, or if they got put in after us. I remember noticing we
were all white in there, the seven of us and the two of them,
and thinking how that was against the odds in Chicago for who
generally gets grabbed by the police. I have a memory of those

two standing up, next to each other, then sitting down with us. I've written some pieces from that experience.

The tank is a big cage, with benches along the sides. There's enough room for the nine of us to sit in two sets facing each other – some of us on their side, some of us across from them. The tank may have smelled like stale beer. They ask us what we're there for, and when we say abortion, they say oooh! Then we ask them. They say they were walking down a sidewalk in Uptown when the cops grabbed them and said they smashed a window and stole a tv set. They say they didn't do it. We don't say one way or the other.

Talking, we learn that one is fifteen years old and five months pregnant. She's wearing jeans and a drawstring blouse under a baseball jacket with pushed up sleeves, and we can see her recently slashed wrists. The stitches are so new the black thread's still there. She says nothing about the cuts but points to cigarette burns on her inner arms and says, I did that to show I could take it. You have to be tough, and you have to prove it. She had her baby's name scratched into her arm like a jailhouse tattoo: Buddy. Even if it's a girl, I'm gonna call it Buddy, she says. That's my brother's name. He's

**in Vietnam. She has a Southern accent and skin so
white her veins look bluer than her tattoo.**

**The other woman is tiny, much smaller than Buddy's
mama, but older. And she's all dressed up, wearing
heels and a long lady-style coat. She has dark red
hair and dark red lipstick, and she doesn't say much.
She smiles almost the whole time and looks sleepy.
Maybe she's a little drunk. Later, she's the one
Denah meets in the elevator, going down to night
court with Angie. She's the one who goes up in front
of the judge right after Denah.**

That's a big moment for Denah, what she sees and hears then.
It's only a moment, but it's deep. And she's kinda stunned.
See, the judge smiles at Denah and calls her Mrs. Al does all
the talking. She just stands there, in front of the high bench.
Her part is to thank the judge. She thinks the judge's voice is
professional-friendly, sober and kindly, like the voice of a judge
is supposed to be, you know?

**He says, You can go now, Mrs. Marcus. You can go
home to your baby. When he says that is when he
smiles.**

She's dulled out from the experiences of the past 20 hours but
she speaks her part.

She says, Thank you, your honor. Then she turns away and walks toward the door with Al, who – now that Denah's free – has taken over Angie's job as elbow guide. This moment I'm talking about is maybe five seconds – not as much as ten. In that moment of seconds, Denah sees with peripheral vision the small woman led to the bench and hears the judge use a different voice. He changes his voice, like you do when you're reading out loud, like to children. He changes it to a scary voice, a bad voice.

To the small woman, he says, You. Look at me when I talk to you.

Denah stops walking, starts to turn. Al's touch on her elbow turns to a grasp, pinching her skin through her sweatshirt. He pulls her forward, and she moves with him; she walks out the door with him.

See – she left the Janes up in the cells and the small woman down in the basement. The breakfast is almost superfluous. It's symbolic – no, wait, what am I saying? No symbolism needed. We'll do it so the audience sees her *get it*, sees her understand what just happened. We need a *really* good actor for this – among the younger ones, who could do it? Is Jennifer Lawrence old enough yet?

Right. Yes. Yes yes yes – I'll keep my cast notes with my music notes. It *is* like the music for me because my mind just goes there, and I start making a list. For the actors it's who've I seen recently, who's the right age and type – and who's got the chops.

Let's have a tea break – I'll put up the kettle on that stove-top – is there any ginger tea in that basket of herbals?

While the water boils, let's think some more about the underneath stuff, the not-plot stuff. I've been thinking about some questions we need to answer: should we have post-bust action in the movie? Do we want anything about what went on in the Service after May 2, 1972? How the other Janes dealt with it? What happened when the Roe decision came down? How much – if anything – do we want to do with the larger context, the whole scene around abortion in the USA at that time?

We seven, called "The Abortion Seven" in the newspapers, spent the next few months going through interviews with lawyers and then working with the lawyer we chose. I have some of those scenes written, but they're scanty. In those months we learned about law, not medicine. Meantime, the Service kept working.

What do you think? Do we want to have those interviews, the little batch of political lawyers the seven women go to see? Each was a story all by itself – we're talking Boccaccio here, *Dubliners*. Flannery O'Conner. Alice Munro! All stories, all the time.

And do we want the one they chose, the Janes' lawyer, to be in the movie? *She* was cinematic. Picture this: she comes to court in canary Yellow pants & a canary Yellow sleeveless sweater, carrying a canary Yellow patent leather briefcase. This is a white woman with a deep tan on her bare arms, and the arms are ringed with silver bangle bracelets; she's wearing matching bangle earrings. I wish I could remember the shoes. Anyway, she was the proverbial sight to behold and, except for us – a pack of smart girls, she was probably smarter than everybody else in the courtroom. Also tougher. So if we need a character, she definitely was one. Also, choosing her was not unanimous, though a grudging consensus was reached – some Jane-on-Jane tension, with Betsy against, Denah for, and a certain amount of negativity in the negotiations.

Another possibility: the Janes took a weekend retreat about a month after the bust – the seven were invited to use a farm up in Wisconsin to decompress and hang out for a few days. Now, in the world of subplots, this is probably too far out, but the fact is — I mean, the *truth* is — in real life the farm was owned by a married couple, and the man had been Denah's lover.

Yeah. Well, you know — real life. I'm sure it seems bizarre, or at least unreal, as reality so often does when you tell it as a story, after it's all done happening. You can imagine people in the theater saying, Sure. Right. Please. But the farm as a scene, a set — that could be useful, no? I mean *if* we decide to go past the bust itself in the chronology of the film, *if* we tell more about the seven in those subsequent weeks? That's why I say we have to answer these questions in front.

Thanks! This tea is lovely, so fragrant.

Here's what else I've got, in notes or full story drafts (I've got characters, plot and dialogue for some of these): some Janes who weren't working that day hit the ground running when they heard, raising money for bail, organizing, figuring out where the women could go who weren't done yet (that day and the rest of the week and the next; we had a couple hundred women waiting) — they did all get done, you know. Every single woman got her abortion.

Plus, I wrote a little about the home front — like, what's going on in the lives of the seven while the bust/jail/lockup stuff is happening. And I made up stories for several people waiting at the front, thinking about the three I already mentioned (Francesca and Shelley and the woman who needed to rest a little before she went back to her husband) plus a typical mix of folks who'd be there – you could probably guess.

And I've got a little bit about the people who'd given their apartment to use that day – every day we worked, people had done that, you know, gone away for the day so we could use their homes – and I made up a story about *those* people, what happens when they find out the Service was busted at their apartment. Which definitely broadens the focus, maybe even diffuses the impact. I just want you to know I've got it – I want you to know everything I've got here, so we can use it if we want to. It's all potential material – stuff that could go under the credits, could be flashback, split-screen, outtakes for a DVD, whatever. Maybe we'll do a mini-series!

Oh hey, there was this guy, a *Daily News* reporter, a totally decent guy, who spotted Denah's name in the police report on the abortion bust and remembered her from the teacher firing. He'd done a long feature then, interviewed her and the other teachers – and wrote a good article with several follow-ups, a *newspaper* mini-series. So he called her.

He'd been in the courtroom that morning when the other six appeared before a different judge and things went pretty much as Al said they would. He asked me if I'd talk with him, or if I'd rather talk to a woman this time. Honest to God, that's what he said! Kinda mournfully but sweetly: I suppose you want to talk to a woman reporter for this?

Yes! There was that time, that tiny time in history, my young friends, when such a thing could and did happen. I said yes, he said okay, and a few minutes later a woman called me, saying, Charlie Atwood just gave me your number, will you talk to me about the Abortion Seven?

More tea, yes, thanks.

Years ago I wrote a pair of scenes, one at a front and one at a place, running parallel in time, but I may have junked it – I can check. In any case, we could certainly put in a little of that for, let's say, a couple minutes max, before the cops show up. Then we could go right into the bust action. That's one option – it'd be easy to recreate, or we could write some new people. No matter what, we should decide how much clinical action to use and how to show it. *If* we show it. Do we show a gamut? Or just some samples? Or what? And when? Like, maybe Denah goes in to see if Shelley's done, so there's a naturally revealed room where an abortion's in progress. We don't want to pander or sensationalize – and we sure don't want to make the mistake that Romanian director made with the fake-looking fetus – the one bad shot in a good movie. I'm assuming you've seen all the relevant films, *Vera Drake, Cider House,* and the new one,

Obvious Child? There's only a handful – so few you could watch them all in one day. Now, why do you suppose that is?

Here's a bit I wrote and never could decide where to put it – I think we should use it; it could work for us because it's dialogue. See if you like it – in the police van or at the station, Betsy says:

> **'Member that meeting when everybody was all up in arms about South Side Sam, the guy with the speculum collection? Was that when Lucy said "life is a movie"? I know, if *my* life is a movie, I'm not the director. I must be the screenwriter because my ideas, and my lines, always get changed and cut. I definitely did not write *this* into it. These hours with the Chicago police would not have been on my list of things to include in the script of my life.**

Betsy has always had some excellent attitude.

Let's talk – at some point – about how much we might need of that kind of thing, dialogue among the seven, emotional interaction among the Janes, stuff that shows how Betsy doesn't much like Denah but understands that her dear friend Claudia does – and her good pal Lucy does, too. We might use the rough deal Mandy has going on, where one of the heavies doesn't like her – no, wait, that actually doesn't matter here! I'll save that for other stories; Mandy's situation as a Jane doesn't play in the plot of the bust, not really. In fact, I bet being one of the seven upped her status in the Service. And besides, I'm going too far into reality – we don't need exclusively real stuff in the movie, so we can make up the relationship parts. Harriet, and her separation from the others, for instance, whatever they think of her and she of them, can just grow out of the plot – we don't need my memories or anybody else's for that stuff.

What if we take a break? Not just a few minutes like these water and tea breaks – I think we should go for a walk, eat food. Are you up for that, or is it just because I'm talking so much I need to change gears? I know you two must be really tired, coming right from the airport, setting up, and then being on the receiving end of all this talk. You should rest, too. Let's turn everything off and get out of here for a while. Let's walk over to the lake.

Nice work on your forearms – I especially like the moon and stars, the way the color was done. Where'd you get it?

Mine were all done here in Chicago except one; this one I got in SanFrancisco from Lyle Tuttle. All of it long before you were old enough to get tattooed, maybe even before you were born. I love saying that! I don't just mean the deliberate use of cliché (enjoyable as that is). I once met a woman on the bus, about as much older than me as I am older than you. She sat down next to me. After she got settled in, she leaned over and looked me over. All over. Then she grasped my thigh and squeezed. Then she twisted sideways to look right into my face, and said, I was getting tattooed before you were born. When the great ones – the inventors of tattoo art in the United States of America – were still working. You know what I mean, girlie?

That really happened.

Judith Arcana

Judith Arcana writes poems, stories, essays and books; her work appears in journals and anthologies online and on paper. Her books include *Grace Paley's Life Stories, A Literary Biography*; the poetry collection *What if your mother*; and the poetry chapbook *4th Period English*. Her most recent publications are a chapbook of poems, *The Parachute Jump Effect* (2012); a prose fiction zine, *Keesha and Joanie and JANE* (2013); and a set of three broadsides, *The Water Portfolio* (2014). In 2013-14, a sandwich was named for her at the lovely and amazing Fleur De Lis bakery/café in Portland. You can listen to Judith read poems on SoundCloud (https://soundcloud.com/judith-arcana) and tell a story at KBOO (http://kboo.fm/content/bearwitnessjuditharcana); for more information and links, visit http://www.juditharcana.com/.

CPSIA information can be obtained
at www.ICGtesting.com
Printed in the USA
LVHW021733200123
737528LV00016B/1791